DIL

NORMAN
PRICE

BELLA
LASAGNE

JAMES

SARAH

MEET ALL THESE FRIENDS IN BUZZ BOOKS:

Thomas the Tank Engine

The Animals of Farthing Wood

Wind in the Willows

Winnie-the-Pooh

Fireman Sam

First published in Great Britain by Buzz Books,
an imprint of Reed Books, Children's Publishing
Michelin House, 81 Fulham Road, London SW3 6RB
and Auckland, Melbourne, Singapore and Toronto

ISBN 1 85591 387 9

Printed in Italy by Olivotto

BIRTHDAY SURPRISE

Story by Rob Lee
Illustrations by The County Studio

It was Station Officer Steele's birthday, but Fireman Sam and Firefighter Elvis Cridlington were pretending that they had forgotten.

"I hope he doesn't know about the surprise party," Elvis whispered to Sam.

6

"Shh," warned Sam, as Station Officer Steele came into the mess hall.

"Any mail for me?" he asked. "Cards or parcels or anything?"

"No sir," Sam replied, hiding a smile.

Sarah and James had taken the bus to Newtown to collect Station Officer Steele's birthday cake from the bakery. They were on their way to the bus stop when it began to rain.

"The cake mustn't get wet!" said James.

"I've got an idea. Let's visit Penny at Newtown Fire Station while we wait for the bus to Pontypandy," said Sarah. "That way we'll stay dry, and so will the cake!"

At Newtown Fire Station, Firefighter Penny Morris made tea for the twins.

"Look at the cake we've got for Station Officer Steele's birthday," said Sarah.

Inside the box was a large cake in the shape of Jupiter, the fire engine.

"Station Officer Steele will certainly like that," Penny laughed. She pointed to a similar box on the table. "I've got a present for him, too, but it's a surprise."

As soon as the rain had stopped, the twins went out to catch the bus to Pontypandy.

"Hurry, James," said Sarah. She held the box in front of her as she ran towards the bus stop. "We don't want to miss it."

But Sarah was running so fast, she slipped on the pavement and the box went flying!

James dived forward and caught the box just as it was about to land in a puddle.

"Oh dear, I'm soaked!" groaned James.

"At least the cake is still dry," said Sarah.

Just then, Trevor's bus appeared.

"Jump aboard, you two," he called. "The Pontypandy Express is at your service."

When Fireman Sam finished his shift at the
fire station he decided to go fishing.

"The rain should bring the fish to the
surface," said Sam to himself. "I'd like to
catch a nice big trout for Station Officer
Steele's birthday dinner."

He waved as he noticed Trevor's bus pass
him on the road alongside Pandy River.

14

Further down, the rain had made the road slippery.

"Watch out!" cried Trevor to the twins.

He tried to stop the bus, but it slid out of control and plunged into the river.

Water poured into the bus.

"Onto the roof, you two!" Trevor told the twins. "The water won't reach up there."

He helped them to clamber out of the bus and onto the roof.

"I'll wade through the river and phone for help," he said.

Sarah and James sat on the roof of the bus and waited. Then Sarah spotted a box floating downstream away from the bus.

"Look, James!" she cried. "The cake will be ruined!"

Downriver, Fireman Sam was not having much luck fishing. Suddenly, he noticed a large box floating towards him.

"Strange," he thought. "I wonder where that came from?"

He pulled the box into the boat. Curious,
he began rowing upriver.

"Great fires of London!" he exclaimed, as
he spotted Trevor's bus in the river.

"That's a funny place to park a bus," said
Sam, as he helped the twins into the boat.
"Are you two all right?"

"Yes, Uncle Sam, we're fine," said Sarah.

James noticed the box in Sam's boat.
"You've found Station Officer Steele's
birthday cake!" he exclaimed.

20

"It might be a bit soggy," said Sam.

Just then, Trevor returned.

"Penny's on her way from Newtown Station," he called. "I'll stay here and help her tow the bus out of the river."

"Righto, Trevor," replied Sam. "I'll take these two back to Pontypandy."

Penny arrived minutes later in Venus, the rescue tender.

"We'll soon have your bus on dry land," she said, and she quickly attached a tow rope from Venus to the back of the bus.

Slowly, she towed the bus onto the road.

22

Trevor climbed into the driver's seat and turned the key. Nothing happened.

"The engine is damp," he said glumly.

"Don't worry," said Penny. "I'll tow you to Pontypandy. We'll be just in time for Station Officer Steele's birthday party. I've already stowed his present in Venus."

That afternoon, Sam and the twins were helping Elvis to get ready for the party.

"First class, Elvis!" said Sam, admiring the food that Elvis had prepared. "It's a good job there's no need for the fish."

"It's a pity the cake is ruined though," groaned James, looking at the soggy box.

"We haven't missed the surprise, have
we?" asked Penny, as she and Trevor
arrived with their presents.

"Not at all," Sam replied.

"Good," said Penny. She held up her box.
It was wrapped up with a big bow. "I hope
Station Officer Steele likes my present."

"Shh! He's coming!" whispered James.

Immediately, everyone was quiet.

"Everyone's forgotten my birthday," they heard Station Officer Steele mutter as he opened the door to the mess hall.

FIREMAN SAM

STATION OFFICER STEELE

TREVOR EVANS

ELVIS CRIDLINGTON

PENNY MORRIS

Station Officer Steele opened the other box to reveal a pair of green wellies.

"We must have swapped boxes!" laughed Penny to the twins.

Fireman Sam chuckled. "This party has been a surprise in more ways than one!"

Penny gave Station Officer Steele her box.

"These are for gardening," she told him.

Station Officer Steele opened the box,
then gave Penny a puzzled look.

"Er, how do I use a cake in my garden?"

"That's our cake!" exclaimed Sarah.

"SURPRISE!!" they shouted. "Happy birthday, Station Officer Steele!"

He beamed.

"So you haven't forgotten after all," he said happily.

27